What Santa Can't Do

NORTH POLE

ALSO AVAILABLE

To all of Santa's
helpers, big and small
—D. W.

To one of Santa's
best helpers, Linda C.
—D. C.

ISBN 0-439-69669-0

Text copyright © 2003 by Douglas Wood. Illustrations copyright © 2003 by Doug Cushman.
All rights reserved. Published by Scholastic Inc., 557 Broadway, New York, NY 10012,
by arrangement with Simon & Schuster Books for Young Readers,
Simon & Schuster Children's Publishing Division. SCHOLASTIC and associated logos are
trademarks and/or registered trademarks of Scholastic Inc.

12 11 10 9 8 7 6 5 4 3 2 1   4 5 6 7 8 9/0

Printed in the U.S.A.   40

First Scholastic printing, November 2004

Book design by Greg Stadnyk
The text for this book is set in 20-pt. Garamond Book.
The illustrations for this book are rendered in pen-and-ink and watercolor.

What Santa Can't Do

WORKSHOP

by Douglas Wood   **pictures by Doug Cushman**

SCHOLASTIC INC.

New York Toronto London Auckland Sydney
Mexico City New Delhi Hong Kong Buenos Aires

There are lots of things that regular people can do, but Santa can't.

He can find every house in every town in every country.

But sometimes he can't find his pipe or his slippers.

He can remember everybody on his list.

But he can't quite remember what Mrs. Claus said
to get at the grocery store.

Santa can never buy enough reindeer biscuits.

He can't drive a car.
(That would hurt the reindeer's feelings.)

And he can't fly in airplanes.
(That would *really* hurt their feelings!)

He can't shave.
No one would know him.

And he can't wear a suit and tie to work.
Well, maybe a *red* suit.

Santa can't quite touch his toes.

Or do as many sit-ups as he used to.

Santa can't wear Bermuda shorts and a T-shirt.
Or sandals.

Santa can't do his best work without elves.

And he can't wait to try out the new toys!

Santa just can't help smiling.

And he can't seem to smile without his eyes twinkling.

He can't *stand* having an empty lap.

Santa can't chuckle. Or giggle. Or snicker.
He can only "Ho! Ho! Ho!"

He can't pack a regular suitcase.

Santa can't sleep at night. At least, not on Christmas Eve!

He can't leave for work without a kiss.
And a present for someone special.

He can't come into a house the normal way.
He doesn't know how doorknobs work.

Santa doesn't really like fires in fireplaces. ("Ouch!")

He just can't seem to walk past a plateful of cookies.
Or a glass of milk.

And he can't leave a single gift in his bag,
even the tiniest one.

There are lots of things Santa can't do.
Lots of ways he's different.
But in one way he's just like you and me.

He can't *wait* for Christmas!